Dear Parent:
Your child's love of reading starts here!

Every child learns to read in a different way and at his or her own speed. Some go back and forth between reading levels and read favorite books again and again. Others read through each level in order. You can help your young reader improve and become more confident by encouraging his or her own interests and abilities. From books your child reads with you to the first books he or she reads alone, there are I Can Read Books for every stage of reading:

SHARED READING
Basic language, word repetition, and whimsical illustrations, ideal for sharing with your emergent reader

BEGINNING READING
Short sentences, familiar words, and simple concepts for children eager to read on their own

READING WITH HELP
Engaging stories, longer sentences, and language play for developing readers

READING ALONE
Complex plots, challenging vocabulary, and high-interest topics for the independent reader

I Can Read Books have introduced children to the joy of reading since 1957. Featuring award-winning authors and illustrators and a fabulous cast of beloved characters, I Can Read Books set the standard for beginning readers.

A lifetime of discovery begins with the magical words "I Can Read!"

Visit www.icanread.com for information
on enriching your child's reading experience.

I Can Read® and I Can Read Book® are trademarks of HarperCollins Publishers.

Flat Stanley and the Bees

Text copyright © 2019 by the Trust u/w/o Richard Brown f/b/o Duncan Brown

Illustrations © 2019 by Macky Pamintuan

www.icanread.com

Library of Congress Control Number: 2018952015
ISBN 978-0-06-236601-6 (trade bdg.)—ISBN 978-0-06-236600-9 (pbk.)

Book design by Honee Jang

19 20 21 22 23 SCP 10 9 8 7 6 5 4 3 2 1   ❖   First Edition

I Can Read!

FLAT STANLEY

and the Bees

created by Jeff Brown
by Lori Haskins Houran
pictures by Macky Pamintuan

HARPER
An Imprint of HarperCollinsPublishers

Stanley Lambchop lived
with his mother, his father,
and his little brother, Arthur.

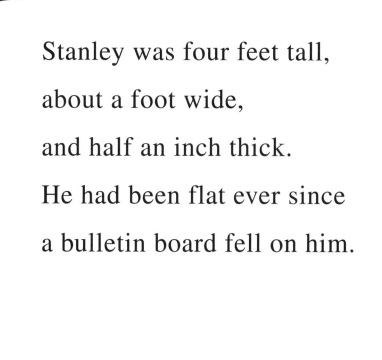

Stanley was four feet tall,
about a foot wide,
and half an inch thick.
He had been flat ever since
a bulletin board fell on him.

Being flat didn't stop Stanley

from eating just as much

as a regularly shaped boy.

"Are the honey buns done?"

he asked one summer afternoon.

"Not yet," said Mrs. Lambchop.

"I don't know why I'm baking.

It's too hot today!"

"We'll cool you off,"

said Mr. Lambchop.

"Boys, let's do the Fan!"

Stanley flung himself on the floor.

Arthur folded him up

like an accordion.

Then Mr. Lambchop grabbed

Stanley by the ankles

and flapped him back and forth.

WHOOSH!

"Much better!" said Mrs. Lambchop.

"Run outside and play, boys.

I'll let you know

when the buns are ready."

"Let's go," said Stanley.

"We can use our new slippy slide!"

Stanley loved the slippy slide.

He always slid faster and farther

than anyone else!

Outside, Stanley and Arthur spotted
Tom and Sam from down the street.
"Want to slide?" called Arthur.
"Sure!" said Tom.

"Let's play tag,"

said Sam after a while.

"Okay," said Stanley. "You're it!"

Stanley loved tag, too.

He could bend and twist

so he was almost impossible to catch.

"How about hide-and-seek?"

Tom suggested next.

That was Stanley's favorite game of all!

He fit into the best hiding places.

"This is perfect!" Stanley thought,

curling up inside a tire swing.

"No one will ever find me!"

Then he heard a sound.

"Eeeek!" someone cried.

Stanley leaned out of the swing.

"Found you!" said Arthur.

"No, you didn't," said Stanley.

"Don't you hear that sound?

I think someone's in trouble."

The boys listened.

"Eeeek!" came the cry again.

Stanley and Arthur followed

the sound up a hill.

Sam hurried after them.

"What's going on?" Sam asked.

Before Stanley could answer,

he heard another sound.

An angry sound.

BZZZZZZZZZZZZZZZZZZ!

"Oh, no!" said Arthur.

"It's Tom!"

Their friend stood like a statue,
too scared to move.

A swarm of bees buzzed around him!

"Arthur!" yelled Stanley.

"Let's do the Fan!"

"Got it!" Arthur said.

Stanley flung himself on the grass.

Arthur folded him up

like an accordion.

Then Arthur grabbed Stanley

by the ankles and tried

to flap him up and down.

But he couldn't do it.

Stanley was too heavy!

Sam rushed over to help.

"One, two, three, FLAP!"

Arthur called.

Together, they fanned Stanley

with all their might.

WHOOSH!

The blast of air blew the bees away!

But not very far.

The boys took off down the hill.

The bees came after them!

"They're catching up!" Tom yelped.

Then Stanley saw something.

The slippy slide!

Stanley let the others

sit on top of him.

WHIZ!

They sailed along

and landed with a wet PLOP

at the Lambchops' back door.

The boys raced inside.

So did the bees!

"Here they come," moaned Arthur.

"Eeeek!" squeaked Tom.

But then . . .

. . . the swarm swerved!

"What? Where—" began Stanley.

Then he gasped.

"THE HONEY BUNS!"

Sure enough, the sweet, sticky buns were covered in sweet, sticky bees.

"Oh, dear!" cried Mrs. Lambchop, walking into the kitchen.

Then Mrs. Lambchop started to laugh.

"It is too hot for warm buns anyway.

You know what we need, boys?"

"Ice cream!"